How Are You Feeling Now?

MOLLY POTTER

ILLUSTRATED BY
SARAH JENNINGS

BLOOMSBURY EDUCATION
LONDON   OXFORD   NEW YORK   NEW DELHI   SYDNEY

Dedicated to my wonderful friend Leilai Immel-Parkinson – one of my favourite playmates who is such a mix of fun, interesting stuff, humour, depth and bizarreness!

BLOOMSBURY EDUCATION
Bloomsbury Publishing Plc
50 Bedford Square, London, WC1B 3DP, UK
29 Earlsfort Terrace, Dublin 2, Ireland
BLOOMSBURY, BLOOMSBURY EDUCATION and the Diana logo are trademarks of Bloomsbury Publishing Plc
First published in Great Britain, 2023 by Bloomsbury Publishing Plc
Text copyright © Molly Potter, 2023
Illustrations copyright © Sarah Jennings, 2023

Molly Potter has asserted her right under the Copyright, Designs and Patents Act, 1988, to be identified as Author of this work

A catalogue record for this book is available from the British Library

ISBN: HB: 978-1-8019-9169-8; ePDF: 978-1-8019-9170-4; ePub: 978-1-8019-9168-1

2 4 6 8 10 9 7 5 3 1

Printed and bound in China by Leo Paper Products, Heshan, Guangdong

To find out more about our authors and books visit www.bloomsbury.com and sign up for our newsletters

How Are You Feeling Now?

Feelings visit us all the time. They are a normal part of being a human!

Some feelings are enjoyable and others are not. We can't stop ourselves from feeling the less enjoyable ones, but we can get really good at knowing what to do when they come along.

This book looks at twelve different feelings. It has ideas for what you can do when you feel each of them, and sometimes suggests ways to help you explore feelings further.

P.S. You might also have the book *How Are You Feeling Today?* This book gives you another set of emotions to think about!

If you are feeling . . .

. . . giggly
turn to page 6.

. . . anxious
turn to page 8.

. . . confused
turn to page 10.

. . . disappointed
turn to page 12.

. . . proud
turn to page 14.

. . . brave
turn to page 16.

...frustrated

turn to page 18.

...guilty

turn to page 20.

...lonely

turn to page 22.

THANK YOU

...grateful

turn to page 24.

...surprised

turn to page 26.

...playful

turn to page 28.

When you feel giggly, you could...

Try out some different ways of laughing and see which sounds the funniest.

Describe what made you giggle and see if it makes you giggle even more.

With a friend, say 'I am extremely serious' in a very serious voice, until you start giggling.

Imagine being a wizard who could cast a giggle spell on other people. Even people on TV!

Decide where you would be on a giggle-ometer.

Pull a really funny face that might make someone else giggle.

Imagine how you could change ordinary things to make people giggle.

Tell a joke to make other people giggle too.

We feel giggly when we think something is funny, or sometimes we just get the giggles for no reason! Remember, it's important not to giggle at other people in a way that might upset them.

When you feel **anxious**, you could . . .

Remind yourself that you have coped before in situations that seem scary.

Imagine everything that you are anxious about turning out well.

Remember that most things do turn out OK – even the things we have been really anxious about.

Do some exercise like star jumps, or go for a walk outside.

Imagine a picture of the thing you feel anxious about and then imagine scrunching it up into a tiny ball.

Find an adult who cares about you and talk to them about why you are anxious.

I am anxious about getting a new teacher.

Use all of your brain to do something you really love.

Imagine smelling a flower. Breath in slowly through your nose to smell it, and breath out even more slowly through your mouth to blow the petals.

We feel anxious when we're not sure how something will turn out. We keep thinking about what could go wrong, and it can feel like we won't be able to cope.

9

When you feel confused, you could...

Work out exactly what you are confused about.

Work out what questions you need to ask to stop you from being confused.

Say 'I am SO confused'. See how long you can say 'so' for!

Write a list of people who are good at explaining things. Tell one of them you're confused and ask for help.

Take photos or draw pictures of people pulling their most confused face to show how everyone gets confused at times.

Imagine you were given a really confusing meal. What meal would that be?

Draw what your confused thoughts would look like.

Tell an adult that you need *clarification* because you are confused. It's fun to use fancy words!

We feel confused when we don't understand something or we can't work out what to do. Being confused can make us feel like we are in a real muddle, and it's not usually enjoyable.

11

When you feel **disappointed**, you could . . .

Sigh or groan again and again until it starts to make you giggle.

Remember a time when you were disappointed and think about how that feeling didn't last for long.

Ask a friend about a time they were disappointed and what happened.

Screw your face up really tightly to show how disappointed you are, until your disappointment starts to disappear.

Find a person, cuddly toy or pet to cuddle.

Give yourself five minutes of quiet time to deal with your disappointment.

Say aloud exactly why you're disappointed.

I'm so disappointed because I was so excited about the beach.

Think about something you are really looking forward to.

We feel disappointed when something we're really excited about doesn't happen, or it isn't as good as we thought it would be. Feeling disappointed can be a mixture of grumpiness, sadness and anger. Luckily, it doesn't usually last too long!

When you feel proud, you could...

Puff up your chest and give yourself a thumbs up.

Tell someone what you are proud of by miming it.

Let me guess ... can you tie your shoelaces now?

Give yourself a mark out of ten for how well you think you did.

I think this is a nine out of ten.

Imagine someone you admire telling you how proud they are of what you did.

I'm very proud of you.

Make a museum display of things you are proud of.

Design and make yourself a badge.

Think of the thing you are most proud of yourself for, even if it is a small thing.

Hand out 'I am proud of you' awards to your friends and family.

We feel proud when we're pleased with something we've done or something we have, or when there is something we like about ourselves. Pride is an enjoyable feeling.

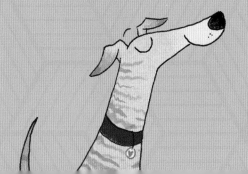

When you feel brave, you could . . .

Decide to learn something new.

Wonder what the recipe for being brave would have in it.

Do something that you would usually find quite difficult.

Imagine that bravery is a shield that protects you from fear. Try drawing that shield.

Remember that being brave is a choice and think about why it's a good choice to make.

I'm so glad I did that.

Write a list of all the things you have managed to do by being brave.

Make up a brave dance or walk.

Think about words that can encourage other people to be brave.

Go on!

You can do it!

We feel brave when we decide to do something that scares us. Feeling brave can sometimes be a struggle, but it can mean we get to try new things and feel proud of ourselves afterwards.

17

When you feel **frustrated**, you could . . .

Tell yourself clearly that you are frustrated and think about why.

Ask someone to help you.

Take some time away and try again later.

Imagine everything turning out well.

Think about what you could say to help someone who is frustrated.

Imagine a monster eating your frustration.

Talk about what feeling frustrated can teach you.

Think about a time when you did something really well. What did you do to get there?

We feel frustrated when we're trying to do something and it just keeps going wrong. Feeling frustrated isn't enjoyable and it doesn't usually help us to achieve what we want.

When you feel guilty, you could ...

Work out exactly what you feel guilty about and how many people it affected.

Think about where inside your body you feel guilty.

See if you can sing 'guilty' in a way that makes you sound really guilty.

Think about which words you could use to describe what it's like to feel guilty.

Think about what you could do to make things better so you feel less guilty.

Think about what you would do differently next time.

Stand how you think guilt would stand if it were a statue.

GUILT

Think about what lessons feeling guilty can teach us.

We feel guilty when we believe we have done something wrong that we think is our fault and we really wish we hadn't done it! Guilt can teach us not to repeat things that upset or annoy other people.

21

When you feel lonely, you could . . .

Remember that everyone feels lonely now and then.

Make a poster of your favourite people and write something you like about each person.

Remind a friend how much you like them by giving them a card filled with compliments.

Paint a picture that looks like loneliness to you.

Try to make a new friend.

Remember nice things people say about you. If you can't remember any, ask the people you love.

Draw a picture of something fun you would like to do with a friend and then try to make it happen.

Look at photos of yourself having fun with friends and family.

We feel lonely when we don't feel understood, connected or close to anyone. We might feel like nobody cares about us, but this is just a thought in our head. Of course lots of people care about us!

When you feel grateful, you could...

Think of something you could thank yourself for today.

Think about what you are grateful for and see if it makes you smile.

Learn how to say 'thank you' in a different language.

Ask some friends what they are most grateful for.

Say 'thank you' to someone who has helped you.

Thank you for helping me Mrs Tiwari.

Make a big 'thank you' poster for the people you live with. Tell each person why they deserve a thank you.

Thank you for the meals you cook for us.

Look around the room and list all the things you are grateful for.

I'm grateful for this snuggly chair.

Make a gratitude diary where you draw something you are grateful for every day.

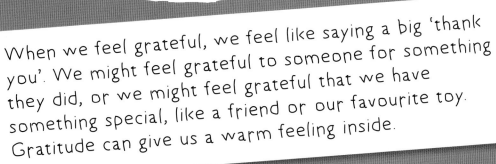

When we feel grateful, we feel like saying a big 'thank you'. We might feel grateful to someone for something they did, or we might feel grateful that we have something special, like a friend or our favourite toy. Gratitude can give us a warm feeling inside.

25

When you feel **surprised**, you could...

Decide whether your surprise was good or not so good.

Try and find a noise that sounds like being surprised.

Imagine what surprise would taste like if it were a drink.

It's fizzy, sour and sweet!

Do a surprised jump.

I was surprised for five seconds when you jumped out at me.

Each time you have a surprise, write down what happened and put it in a jar. Watch it fill up with surprises!

Think how many seconds your surprise lasted for.

I made this face!

Draw some surprised faces and decide which one looks the most surprised.

Tell someone else about your surprise. Show them the face you made when you were surprised.

We feel surprised when something happens that we really didn't expect. Sometimes surprises are fun and enjoyable, but sometimes they can shock us. We usually really notice surprises!

When you feel **playful**, you could . . .

Keep a balloon up in the air for as long as possible.

Draw a picture or write a secret message and hide it for someone to find.

Get dressed and make as many mistakes as possible. Put your clothes on inside out, back to front and upside down!

Pretend to be two animals at once and see if a friend can guess the animals.

28

Pretend to be an alien! Make up a funny language and find someone to talk to.

Make some paper eyes and stick them on things around the house.

Make up funny 'would you rather' questions to ask people.

Would you rather have ears like an elephant or a neck like a giraffe?

Give both of your feet a name and a voice and get them to talk to each other.

What's your favourite type of shoe?

Wellies, definitely.

Feeling playful is an enjoyable emotion because we feel full of fun. It's a feeling that makes us want to play and sometimes be a bit silly!

Notes for grown-ups

Identifying feelings

Like my other book *How Are You Feeling Today?*, this book looks at twelve emotions that children often experience and gives them ideas for what they can do when they feel each emotion. The value in your child using this book not only lies in them thinking about how to express their emotions, it also lies in the process of them trying to identify what they might be feeling. This process will help improve your child's emotional intelligence.

What is emotional intelligence?

When someone is emotionally intelligent they can:
- Notice their emotional responses as they arise.
- Identify what emotion they are feeling.
- Recognise what triggered their different emotions.
- Expect to feel both enjoyable and unenjoyable emotions and accept this as part of being human.
- Understand that emotions give us messages that are sometimes helpful and sometimes unhelpful.
- Express what they are feeling in a way that does not make situations worse.

Why is emotional intelligence a good thing?

A child with good emotional intelligence will find life easier to navigate than a child without it. They will grow up to be at a lower risk of developing depression and anxiety, have an easier time building relationships, be more creative in any moment, be better at maintaining their wellbeing, perform better in tasks that involve others, will be perceived as more confident... and much more.

If we are not aware of our emotions and their impact, it can either mean we engage in behaviours that make situations worse or we become so caught up in the thoughts relating to an emotion that we fail to act at all. If we do not develop emotional intelligence, then emotions control us. But if we do develop emotional intelligence, we learn to manage our emotions.

Ten top tips for helping your child develop emotional intelligence

1) Acknowledge emotions

In a world that mostly values rational thinking, emotions often get ignored despite their potential to have a huge impact on how we function. Help your child understand that emotions are a normal part of being human and we all have them. This might seem obvious, but acknowledging this helps your child start to be more consciously aware of their emotional responses.

2) Consider both enjoyable and unenjoyable emotions.

Help your child to understand that it's normal to feel both enjoyable and unenjoyable emotions. It is completely unrealistic

30

to describe different emotions, e.g. excited – fizzy, sad – a sinking feeling, worried – twitchy and unable to concentrate on anything other than your worries.

5) Use 'emotional check-ins'

You can improve your child's emotional intelligence quite quickly by doing 'emotional check-ins'. This is where you and your child think about what they're feeling, or what they have been feeling, that day. For example at bedtime, you could use a poster showing a variety of emotions to prompt your child to reflect on the emotions they have experienced that day. This will help them improve their emotion vocabulary as well as their ability to recognise feelings.

6) Taking a 'pause'

Emotions can have a powerful impact on what we think and how we behave. Because we rarely make good choices when we are in the grip of a powerful emotion (e.g. anger, shame or panic), it's always a good idea to take time out before we react. Once your child has started to recognise emotions as they arise, teach them to take a pause before reacting, such as counting to ten when they're angry. This can make the difference between a reaction that triggers destructive responses or one that helps to sort a situation out. Remember, we can't always help what we feel, but we can learn to choose how we behave, whatever we are feeling.

to think that we can feel happy all of the time – even if it sometimes feels like the world tells us that is what we should be doing. Trying to ignore or distract your child away from negative emotions does not teach your child how to manage them. Suppressing negative emotions does not make them disappear, but instead means we have less control over them.

3) Consider how you label emotions

Never describe emotions as 'good' or 'bad'. It's better to think of them as enjoyable or unenjoyable. If you tell your child that being angry or jealous is bad, this will mean they will not only feel these emotions, but they will also feel shame for feeling them. If you tell your child that being happy is good, they may try to appear happy often to get your approval, and feel shame if they don't manage it. Healthy emotions come and go without the added complication of these secondary emotions and judgements.

4) Link physical symptoms to each emotion

Some children struggle to identify what they are feeling because they don't know how to link their physical reactions to different emotions. Discuss the physical symptoms of different emotions to help your child recognise each emotion more fully. For example when a person feels angry, their heartbeat tends to speed up, their face might go red and they might clench their teeth and fists. You can also use adjectives and phrases

9) Discuss coping strategies

Help your child learn coping strategies that work for them when they are experiencing strong, unenjoyable emotions. These will be different for each individual and emotion but some common coping strategies for worry and anger can include:

•**Worry:** find out more information about what's causing worry, break the situation and the solutions into small, manageable steps, or practise relaxation techniques or visualisation exercises.
•**Anger:** take time out until the anger subsides, count down from ten, or practise breathing exercises.

7) Taking responsibility for what they feel

Help your child understand that two people can have exactly the same experience (e.g. be insulted) but that this can trigger different emotional responses depending on a variety of factors, such as their sensitivity, what has happened earlier, how they feel about the person who insulted them, how resilient they were feeling at the time, etc. It helps us to understand that we are mostly responsible for our own emotional reactions. Try and help your child not to blame others for their emotional responses as this rarely helps. Encourage them to use 'I messages' to express how they feel, e.g. 'I feel angry when people tease me' instead of, 'You made me angry'. It's a good idea to encourage your child to look inwards and be curious and interested in their emotions and their triggers, rather than to look for someone to blame for how they feel.

8) Learning to empathise

Help your child to empathise when others are having an emotional reaction – even if the other person's emotional 'outburst' is making them uncomfortable. If your child can imagine another person's feelings, they are more likely to be able to help. You can develop your child's empathy by discussing how characters might feel in stories or films as well as talking about situations their friends might be struggling with.

10) Support your child through uncomfortable emotions

You might feel a temptation to distract or 'cheer up' your child when they are experiencing uncomfortable emotions. It is more helpful for your child to 'sit with' uncomfortable emotions without panic. Many achievements or things we have to deal with in life require us to bear uncomfortable emotions, so help your child accept these feelings by providing a safe, secure, calm and loving presence while they are experiencing them. You can talk about what they are feeling and why, but be sure to allow the emotion to run its course and use it as a valuable opportunity to help your child develop resilience.